DATE DUE			

OTHER LIVES

Peter Oresick

ADASTRA PRESS

ISBN 0-938566-29-6
First Edition May 1985
Second Printing September 1985

Thanks are due the following editors of the publications in which these poems, often in earlier versions, have appeared:

The Bellingham Review: About My Son & Hands
The Christian Century: The Jeweler; Annointing the Sick; Old Shevchenko
Michigan Quarterly Review: Receiving Christ
The Minnesota Review: Shooting the Governor of Wisconsin
Pig in a Pamphlet: Tolstoy in Heaven
Pig in a Poke: Last Things
Poetry East: Poem for Hamid
Poetry Northwest: Jump
Sez: Agnes McGurrin
Slow Loris Reader: May Songs
Sojourners: Burial Chant
Willow Springs: How My Brother Came to Love Lenin

I also want to thank the Pennsylvania Council on the Arts for a fellowship which aided me in completing this collection.—P. O.

ADASTRA PRESS
101 Strong Street, Easthampton, MA 01027

for Stephanie

History is the essence
of innumerable biographies.
—Thomas Carlyle

Contents

IV.

I.

Agnes McGurrin

May your death cause no one pleasure.
—Irish proverb

She can't sleep.
After ten years in a shirt factory
and a marriage of 40 years,
after kids, strikes, boredom—
        more kids.
After grandkids, after stroke,
after St. Jude's Home for Diocesan Infirmed,
she can't sleep.
Only this: an image

of late August, a maple losing its leaves.
Her children look consumptive. Thin as twigs.
Here's a table, a bee, a bushel of pears.
They peel easily, smell sweet.
She reaches for a jar and her breasts fall
plump and fragrant into the bushel.
The bee circles her head, Agnes hurries
to finish canning. Her breasts fall again:
pears, more pears . . .
She's flustered, the bee still circling,
then it lights on her wrist. Winter blooms
white as an orchid; a wind stings her awake.

These mornings
her husband drops her roughly into the wheelchair.
Soon he's gone to play cards.
A morning game, pensioners only.
She remembers the club young. Battle of bands.
There was swing, then a slow number.
Lots of smoke and hugging. They'd come early
to see the sand sprinkled on the dance floor.
A handful of sugar to make it smooth.

Agnes starts a letter to her daughter.
She wants to write about *purpose*, but
two cardinals sing from tomato stakes. She's gone
rolling down the wide aisle of her garden.
The birds fly. She begins the ritual
watering, plunging her cupped hand again and again
into the pail, relaxing her fingers over the beans.

Agnes thinks to herself.
A neighbor's phone rings. A bus rumbles past.
She can hardly hear herself,
just a TV preacher voice
through an open window, singing.

The Jeweler

He always repaired a cross & chain free.

Once he outfitted our basketball team
with Holy Infant of Prague medals;
they were the difference, he insisted,
in '37 against Frackville.
He was floating in for a lay-up
when a number 22, a Methodist, grabbed his chain
and choked him silly.
He got so angry
he changed the score by himself.

Someone told me he worked in the mill one day.
Just walked out.
Left for watch repair school in Scranton.

On his gravestone is carved a small clock
and on each side a flowering vine.
At least that's how his brother, a sandblaster,
has worked it out. Before the last trumpet
that clock should ring and ring and ring.

Anna Marie

She has missed Mass again.
She fries pork for Sunday dinner
and her 7-year-old can see her halo
sucked into the exhaust fan.
The other kids wrestle in the den
while the oil sizzles.
The nerves of her breaded hands twitch.

At dinner
she hates how her husband chews
with an open mouth, breathing heavily.

By the time she's scoured the last pan
the kids are back from the alley shouting
about a dead pigeon
and how its body is opening out.
They want permission to bury it
in the rose bed, and she says okay,
just get out.

Her husband's already asleep
under the paper, the TV on,
his mouth open.
She stares for minutes
before poking him awake.

Jump

for S. E. Hinton

I started to say something: the fountain, the film of ice
The park's a good place 2 a.m.—nobody but my partner
I said, "Ain't you bout to freeze to death, Johnnykid?"
A blue Mustang was circling the park, slowly

The park's a good place 2 a.m.—nobody but my partner
"You ain't a wolfin," he said, rubbing his bare arms
A blue Mustang was circling the park, slowly
I need a cigarette, I need a cigarette

"You ain't a wolfin," he said, rubbing his bare arms
"Here they come!" Smelled like whiskey & English
    Leather
I need a cigarette, I need a cigarette
Johnnykid's hand went to his back pocket, his
    switch—

"Here they come!" Smelled like whiskey & English
    Leather
I started to say something: the fountain, the film of ice
Johnnykid's hand went to his back pocket, his
    switch—
I said, "Ain't you bout to freeze to death, Johnnykid?"

The TV Anchor

overworks herself,
and sometimes under the blue-heat
of the lights she's so tired . . .
the arson-for-profit story blurs
with the ghost employee story,
with the massage parlor murders,
then blurs again.

The cameraman wants her blouse unbuttoned
one lower than the weathergirl's on Channel 6,
but she gnashes her fine white teeth at him.

Undercover once, she outdid herself
with a white slavery story.
On camera:
held a handgun so well the pimp squirmed.
Enter the cops . . . exit reporter,
with three girls down the backsteps to safety.

Illegal as it was, no one sued.
Harriet Tubman, they called her,
"A little righteousness and a lot of gun."
Church groups, feminists, PTA's,
all wanted her to speak, wanted to see her
stiff way of holding her head,
the way her blazing eyes never blinked.
As if tomorrow she could kill a man,
then live happily among cloistered women.

Old Shevchenko

I recall him, plainly, in his black wool suit
and his yellow shirt buttoned at the collar.

After evening bells, he'd stroll
until dark, and at corners
he'd quote from the Gospel; a mumble
on the breeze, an angel in black,
drawing laughs from passersby.

I saw him once encircled by *Los Barbados*,
seven bearded men on motorcycles. He glared
at their skull and bone insignias.
Pocketing his bifocals, he unbuttoned his shirt
and doffed his black fedora. From his neck
he lifted a block of painted wood—
the image of the Black Madonna.

It dangled
from a boot lace, then he shook it at them
and passed from their midst unharmed.

This was in the '60s, when I was a boy,
and given to searching for signs. I looked
to the sky, to crumbling gray clouds,
where the blue appeared like a beautiful eye.

I sat and looked around me
and listened. The leaves overhead
scarcely rustled; by their delicate noise
I have trusted my life.

Annointing the Sick

"There is no God," Father Korba said,
"like the silence of a man's own house."
Old Shevchenko, mostly bones, lay there dead.
"God is here," Korba said.
The widow set a table: candles, salt, and bread.

Half the night we sat with her
till I began to drowse:
my mind a wide cloud, passing from the head
through the rooms of the silent house.

II.

St. John of Damascus, a Father of the Church and one of her major poets, wrote during the eighth century at the St. Saba Monastery in Palestine. There he organized the voluminous service books of the Eastern Church and composed numerous poetic Canons, Stichera, Odes, Troparia, and Theotokia. The following three poems were adapted from such texts.

Burial Chant

Where is the crowd and its clamor?
Where is lust for the world?
Where is the ephemeral dream?
All is dust, all ashes, all shadow.

*

What glory does not fade?
What endures unmingled with grief?
Substance is less than shadow,
more deluding than dreams.
In a moment all is struck down.

*

Now I know wisdom: I am dust and ashes.
I search among the graves, see the bones
    laid bare.
Which is the king and which his warrior?
Which is the martyr and which his
    executioner?

*

What mystery befell us?
We wail and grieve at our beauty
bruised in the tomb.
Who surrendered us to corruption?

*

We stand over the graves
of our lost, our bodies entwined
by mysterious wind—
Christ murmuring: *trust*, *trust*.

On Behalf of a Man Whose Soul Is Departing and Cannot Speak

Like drops of rain
    my evil days, and few vanish
in the summer's heat.
    O Lady, save me.

*

Who are these circling me, gaping?
    What do they want?
Save me, O Pure One,
    and crush their teeth and jaws.

*

Mother of Christ, turn
    your ear to me.
When you hear my last groan,
    be faster
than the Evil One's hand.

*

In the distance I always saw this day
    and could have brooded over it.
But only now this weeping,
    so you won't forget me.

*

O Lady, Tormentor
    of the Prince of the Air,
let me pass over unhindered
    as I abandon the earth.

*

No one saves me now.
    There is nothing to save.
O Lady, come
    or I am booty
in the enemy's vault.

*

As you enter first, guardian angel,
    bend your rarefied knees
and cry to Him: "Mercy!
    Don't crush or damn
whom You've labored to shape."

*

Look down, Mother of God,
    that I may see you,
and leap from the body
    laughing, shouting praise.

*

My flesh leaves its bone,
      my joints loosen.
The body and all Nature
      will collapse.

*

If I escape
      the thugs without bodies,
  if I rise
      through abysses of air
and enter . . .
      for ages and ages
I'll praise you, Mother,
      Gate of Heaven.

*

How will I see the invisible?
      How will I open my eye?
Will I survive the vision
      when I see the Master
who, since my youth,
      I've caused grief?

*

On quitting the body,
      I, who have ruined the temple,
can only beg you, Temple of Christ.
      May my spirit escape
the outer dark.

Prayer When Approaching Your Bed

This bed—is it my grave?
Or will the sun blaze again
and uncover me, the condemned soul?

No, this is a grave.
Look in the corner, there's Death.
But it's suffering that I fear,
and judgment.
Still I love evil.

Save me, Lord,
whether I desire it or not.
If You save the just,
if You favor the pure,
it is nothing.
They have earned grace.
Prove You love all
by saving me, Lord,
and may my evil heart not overcome
Your kindness.

III.

Zishe, the Yiddish Samson

I, Zishe, a blacksmith's son, drinking no wine, growing the seven locks of my hair, have always known that I am Samson. Once as a boy, seeing an anti-Semite's dog assume the form of a lion, I snapped its neck with my two good hands, with my cry, *Shema Yisroel!*

At Father's smithy I pumped the bellows: each spark torched the tails of the three hundred foxes; again I sent them into the standing grain and olive orchards of the Philistines.

Though I remember the gouged eyes, the bronze fetters, the millstone heavy as shame, this legacy must pass. This is why I travel the theater circuit and twist iron and bite chains. I will lay prone tonight once more, watch the pallet, the team of horses lowered on me, and raise it, slowly, to the chant of the *Kol Nidre*.

Thus my name grows, thus my enemies grow. I have, praise the Almighty, overcome them. My enemies must admit, through clenched teeth, that I, Zishe, son of Yithak Tsvi Breitbart, the Jew from Lodz, am the strongest man in the world. The gentiles detest me, this Jew who takes the crown of strength from them, but there is nothing they can do about it.

Tolstoy in Heaven

The full shoulders and bosoms
of women in low-necked gowns
are not a problem here.

His other lust? God?
Like two bears in one lair,
Lev Nikolayevich and He.

Look at them playing cards.
Tolstoy, in dead earnest,
holds his cards like a live bird.

Hands like these, forever . . .

Shooting the Governor of Wisconsin

It is not madness
but the high price of milk that prompts the
man.
A bittern sounding like a cow,
an image of tank trucks dumping milk,
have kept him sleepless for weeks.
He is quite sane and deeply believes
in free access to milk.
But his uncle sold the family farm
to Japanese investors.
A gun to him is a tiny engine
of change, while a governor sounds muffled,
melancholy as a cow locked in a shed.
So he squeezes the trigger, gently and quickly.

Press Conference

From the President's mouth fall
six pearls, two roses, a large diamond.
More questions. He replies:
wheat, corn, an infinite number of potatoes.

An aide walks on with a gunnysack.
The President nods,
pulls out a woman's head.
Flies cluster like a black wimple.

Foreign correspondents rush out aghast
and the liberals storm out on principle.
"What does this mean?" reporters shout.
The President answers: two vipers and a toad.

How My Brother
Came To Love Lenin

It was like the pucker
for pickled herring—his face sour
yet chewing persistently

as if to impress a young woman
and her mother across the table.
He gulped the glass of water

before the second helping slipped
seductively down, the woman grinned,

and his intrigued belly
with its more clear brain
signalled the arm to reach again: fish,

water, fish, leaving the tongue
addicted—water, fish—
to the obstinacy of its salt.

Poem for Hamid

1.
Dawn: the sky whitens.
All night the blue factories clanked & whirred,
    thickening the air.
Yet this is a morning,
and this is a grapefruit, this sugar.
This is a key, a car; this is torque
and we move.

This is North America. Have a nice day.
This is not hell, it's a supermarket.
See the lettuce: bib, leaf, iceberg, romaine.
This is not death, it's fried chicken.
Taste it. It has taste.

2. Letter from Abroad, May 1981
The left disappears. Many are underground and the prisons are full. Some mornings the gunshots wake us. Fadwa will rush out of bed, dress, chatter about getting work, but I linger. I am writing leaflets, translating, smoking too much. No word yet from Ali. Mother worries and busies herself cooking.

3.
Remember the time we were taken to jail?
Posting leaflets illegally.
Getting out by morning—my only concern—
    while you were lost in study:
how two kids in for robbery paced,
how they couldn't fill out the forms.
Drunk or dumb? What did it matter?
I think of the green walls peeling,
the one toilet, the chill that floated in
    from the hall.
What makes you believe
everyone lives to some purpose?

4.
That is my son
        pulling himself up on the chair leg.
That is his word, *bup*, sailing
in this comfortable room.
What here is not to like?
What?

5. Letter from Ali, July 1981
I am living in a northern province. No running water, no electricity, nothing like the undergraduate life I loved in Denver. The new regime has no influence here. I am hidden by a good family; from my window I watch them going about each day. The women must knock away shit with a stick before drawing water. Crops are poor. Oil does us little good without rainfall. Some days I wonder how we'll change what the centuries have not touched.

6.
Hamid, that your grief were my life
or my life your grief, is academic.
The lawn fertilizer I do not buy
may never reach your country.
We do what we can. No regrets.
This is still a life, not grief.
Still life.

A Central American Story

Page B9
under a Gimbels ad:
VIDEO DISCS, $20
Altered States, *Rocky III*,
An Officer and a Gentleman.

But my story concerns six rural priests.
In Tarapaca Regiment Headquarters
they'd been blindfolded, lined up,
for preaching some agrarian reform.
An officer placed his pistol
in the first mouth, then fired.
And so on down the line . . .

Do you recall in *Romeo and Juliet*
where Mercutio is slain
and Romeo avenges himself on Tybalt,
lunging with a sword?
"For Mercutio's soul
Is but a little way above our heads,
Staying for thine to keep him company."

I imagine each priest like that,
his ghost lingering a little way above—
quiet as smoke—until the last is shot.
The six then flock like dark birds,
ascending through the ceiling

All of this came to me in 1983
while sitting on the sofa.
My sons were sprawled on the floor
repairing a starship, rapping on it
with wooden spoons.

IV.

Aunt Sophie: Widowed

Pittsburgh, Toledo, Chicago, Detroit.
Uncle Paul changed mills like shoes,
Aunt Sophie dragging behind, dragging
their six weepy daughters.
He ended finally in Kansas, in General Motors,
where his bad heart caught up to him.

My cousins called the priest,
the undertaker, and the doctor,
who gave Sophie a little something.

It was November then.
The stars could barely shine
through the Presbyterian heavens.
Somehow desire like a cyclone
swept over the prairie, over her flat life,
confused her.
                She walked out
naked into a field beyond the garage.
Threw herself flat.
Embraced the earth without a tear,
when a neighbor
huddled Sophie under a coat
and walked her back to the dim house.

Last Things

First there is death, then judgment
Father Korba told me this;
in a moment we will change.

You already know, he grinned,
how in a moment
your life has changed.

Raised up, we will shine.
Time will have snapped, tension
vanished, and we'll shine.

How old will the new body look?
If Grandma looks twenty,
who will know her? And

what if you're Eddie Shepansky
who lost a leg in Vietnam?
Father said, "I said a *new* body."

Time will snap.
The doors of the universe closed
we'll see more clearly:

history like a film upon a screen.
All things will be made known,
no secret too dark.

So what's the point
of the body breaking, this suffering?
It's just a test

for the eternal weight of glory.
Time will have snapped, he said.
Imagine a steel ball the size of the sun

and a hummingbird circling it,
barely grazing it with one wing.
The time it takes to wear it down.

Receiving Christ

after St. John Chrysostom

Not like Judas with a kiss,
but like the good thief
whose broken bones rejoiced.

"The glory of God,
that God *be* God,
is that the poor live."

It is a circumcision
made without hands:
sloughing off the body of flesh,
putting on the body of Christ.

" The glory of God,
that God *be* God,
is that the poor live."

It is to stand
like good Nicodemus and accept the body
as it is lowered from its cross.

May Songs

1.
Stained glass: Our Lady
of Light lances the smoked air.
You study
the side altar, the woman
draped in blue.

Holy places should draw out
the best in us.
Mrs. Chasko,
more still than the marble
Virgin, pray for us.

2.
After we stumble
across two doe, the hillside bursts
into phlox, monk's hood,
trillium. "Like a wedding,"
you say. And within a ring

of willows, mayapple
throngs like a fundamentalist
revival. You lift their skirts
to see if the blossoms
are still intact.

3.
At home our window
channels light tumbling in
torrents that turn slack,
amber as syrup coating
your tenting belly. Beneath

is the dried apple
face of our dreams. When I lay
my hand on your stomach,
always that long calm, then
the baby quickens.

4.
I want to spraypaint
our names, love, on an overpass.
Or lock our initials
in the whitewashed heart
on Second Avenue's mill wall.

Hurry, while the moon
is still low, while the coal sack
clouds mosey across the night. Love,
we've lost ourselves; at each breath
I am more happy.

Meditation in Late Spring

The spinach refuses to sprout.
From the mailbox *Newsweek* is chanting,
Reagan's Arms Buildup, Arms Buildup, Arms.

Too hot, no clouds. Henry loves this
and lies on a beach towel in the driveway.
He's laid off, collecting $175 weekly,

talking lottery or the virtue of wheat germ
to pass the days. I weed and hoe
feeling a little superior

because I'm home by choice, because
I'm raising kids, broccoli, tomatoes,
but I know better. The Lord is probably pleased

with him, his sunning and petty gambling,
even his bodily functions like
existential prayers. I weed and hoe.

Overhead a jet descends,
and the gate rattles, the fence rattles,
the pea vines quiver as well.

Some days I can see God dimly.
Some days we would talk
but for the pane of glass between us.

At the Jewish Cemetery in Carrick

Someone is looking for us.
I sensed it earlier at the creek
while floating on my back, and again
on Route 8 near Brookline.
So we've detoured to this hillside
eroding and crazy with markers.
We're looking for row *mm* or *nn*
or something like that.
I lug the baby; my wife runs ahead.
This neighborhood knows her—
she passes so easily between stones.
She finds the grave, her father
dead ten years now. In the time it takes
to say *kaddish* the sun drops.
I set down my son
and he crawls in the twilight
toward the headstone. Pulls himself up.
His hands read the marble like braille.

Quickly he rounds its corner.
      Vanishes.
I think: *grass*, *stone*, *quiet*—
then babbling from another world.

About My Son & Hands

This month, our son's fourth, he is studying hands
with much reverence and drooling. The books insist
on *more dangling toys, a spoon to play with,*
but the little man prefers a father's knuckle
or a mother's sweet thumb, and especially the joining
of his own two hands. The clumsy fingers of one
explore
those of the other; the grasp, the squeezing
tell him they are dear friends for life.
From his walker his supple spine *dahvens.*
He raises his hands like a rabbi:
a long ceremonious moment . . . then drops them
to his toothless smile, his consonant laugh.
When he rests them on his yellow tray,
it is with authority. The hands emissaries now
ready to accept the small objects we offer.

Colophon

TYPE is 12 point Garamond Old Style with 36 point on the cover and title page. Poem titles are set in an antique face: 18 point Bernhard Booklet.

The First Printing consisted of 275 copies handset, handfed letterpress printed with handsewn signatures glued into a paper cover. 25 copies were handbound in cloth over board and signed & numbered by the author.

The Second Printing used photo-plates of the original page proofs, corrected. The printing for this edition was offset with perfect binding.

Covers for both editions were handprinted on letterpress. The First Printing has 3 colors with solid lino-block cut figures. The Second Printing has 2 colors with the original block cuts hollowed out to produce line figures.

All design, layout and letterpress work by Gary Metras at the Adastra Press.